Originally published in the United States in 2015
by Little, Brown and Company
a division of Hachette Book Group, Inc.

First published in Great Britain in 2015
by Orion Children's Books
an imprint of Hachette Children's Group
a division of Hodder and Stoughton Limited

Carmelite House
50 Victoria Embankment
London EC4Y 0DZ
An Hachette UK Company

1 3 5 7 9 10 8 6 4 2

A catalogue record for this book is available from the British Library.

ISBN 978 1 5101 0082 4

Printed in China

www.orionchildrensbooks.com

Thank You and Good Night

Patrick McDonnell

Orion
Children's Books

The sun set,
the moon rose,

and Maggie helped Clement
button his favourite pyjamas–
the ones with the blue and white stripes.

"We're here!" announced Jean
and his friend Alan Alexander.

Jean's pyjamas had feet in them.

Alan's pyjamas seemed a little too big.

"Surprise!" said Maggie.

"Wheeee!" said Jean.

"Hooray!" said Clement.

"Oops!" said Alan.

"Now what?" Jean wondered.
"Is it time for bed?" Clement asked.
"No," Alan declared.

Alan taught the chicken dance.

Clement won the funny-face contest.

The three friends played hide-and-seek,

again and again.

"Is it time for bed yet?" asked Clement.

"No, no, no," Alan replied.

They bounced the balloon about,

practiced yoga,

and had a little something good to eat.

They studied the night sky,

saw a shooting star,

and made a wish.

A night bird sang a lullaby.

"Sweet sleep,

Sweet sleep,

Sweet sleep."

"Gee, I'm getting sleepy," Jean sighed.

"Gee, I'm getting sleepier," Alan mumbled.

"Gee, I'm already asleep," Clement yawned.

"Now is it time for bed?" they all asked quietly.

"Yes," said Maggie.

Everyone got ready.

They sleep-walked down the hall…

…and snuggled under the blankets.
"Will you tell us a story?" they asked.

"Once upon a time…" Maggie started.

"Ooh, that's a good one!" exclaimed Alan Alexander.

"Hush," whispered Clement.

Maggie read them their favourite bedtime stories—

stories about a majestic elephant,

a brave bear,

and a quiet bunny…

Stories that bring sweet dreams.

"Now, before we go to sleep, let's all say
what we were thankful for this day."

The sun, the moon,
a red balloon.
Hiding, seeking,
fun with friends,
a shooting-star wish
that it never ends.
Cozy pyjamas,
a happy surprise,
night birds singing
sweet lullabies.
Bedtime stories,
old and new,
read with love,
to me,
by you.

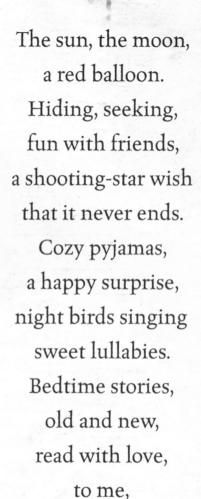

A long, long list
of that and this,
ending with
a good night kiss.

"Thank you."

"Thank you."

"Thank you."

And good night.